BONES

Selected Reviews of David Osborn's Previous Novels

The Last Pope

"A truly great novel. I plan to make it my finest motion picture."

—Martin Poll, producer of *The Lion in Winter*, starring Peter O'Toole and Katharine Hepburn

"A thrilling blend of history, religion, and human relationships."

—*The New York Post*

The Glass Tower

"Breathless introduction to the inner workings of big business …"

—*The Times* Literary Supplement

"[An] institution story perfected by Zola and none the worse for it … deftly, excitingly told."

—*The Daily Telegraph*

"A sharp and entertaining first from Mr. Osborn, who is already an accomplished screenwriter."

—*Lincolnshire Evening Telegraph*

Murder on Martha's Vineyard

"A good tale of mystery and murder. Its plot twists and turns in and out of an intriguing whodunit that packs a punch at the end powerful enough to floor one."
—*Western Morning News*

"This is the first entry in what might become a promising new series.... Osborn has created an interesting protagonist."
—*Publishers Weekly*

Murder on the Chesapeake

"Satisfying tale ... intrepid sleuth."
—*Publishers Weekly*

"The tale is spun tightly and the main characters are engaging."
—*Chicago Sun Times*

Open Season

"A truly brilliant novel ... an accomplished writer in all media, but ultimately a pro ... a superbly organized book, brutal, chilling, but carrying a terrible conviction."
—*Canberra Times*

"This well-plotted thriller makes compulsive holiday reading."
—*Salisbury Journal*

BONES

A NOVELLA

DAVID OSBORN

Published by Dagmar Miura
Los Angeles
www.dagmarmiura.com

Bones

This is a work of fiction. Names, characters, businesses, places, events, and incidents are either the products of the author's imagination or used in a fictitious manner. Any resemblance to actual persons, living or dead, or actual events is purely coincidental.

First published 2024

ISBN: 979-8-89195-013-9

To all in my family

Ode to a wonder of the past

Now listen to the whistle, the rumble,
    and the roar,
As she dashes thro' the woodland, and
    speeds along the shore,
Stand back as she comes thundering
    like a fiery meteor,
It's the mighty locomotive of the
    Wabash Cannonball.

One

The U.S. postal van pulled up sharply before a blue rural mailbox identified in small white letters on its side as 24 Holway Road. The driver, a veteran postal delivery employee named Spencer Carling, fetched a handful of letters and junk mail held together with a rubber band that he'd separated from others earlier that day, deftly delivered it into the box, and drove away with only a brief glance at the small stone house the mail box served.

Set against a small grove of birch trees and with a freshly mowed lawn that held back surrounding fields, it was reached by a narrow driveway wedged here and there between occasional apple trees, and was a small structure with steep slanted dark slate roofs. Little shuttered windows were on each side of the front door, above which another room on the second floor huddled under a nearly obscuring gable.

Uninhabited for as long as Spencer Carling could remember, it had always been known as "The Haunted House" because, it was said, someone had once been murdered in it, and it was only ever visited by teenagers expressing high spirits by vandalizing or even by breaking into its interior to hold drinking, drugs, and sex parties amidst the faded remnants of its furniture.

That had been in years past. The house and its surrounding property was now quite different in appearance than when Spencer began delivering mail to its new owner, who had bought it two years ago.

Until then, weeds had largely obscured its driveway as well as the short flagstone walk from a nearby small dilapidated barn to the front door. Unwanted ugly vines climbed up the stone sides of the house itself, while the paint on the shutters of its small windows had peeled away. And brush had begun to cover up what had once been the mowed lawn of its one-acre property surrounded by the fields and woods that separated it from other semirural residences around the town of Connors Falls.

That had all changed with its new owner. The sagging roof of the little barn was repaired, flowers bordered the gravel driveway, fresh paint adorned the shutters of windows, and ugly climbing vines had been removed, while the disappearance of brush on the surrounding lawn had revealed a small brook crossing a far end of the property. A pickup truck was now parked at the end of the driveway close to the front door.

Spencer had watched with something close to awe as life returned to the little house, and he daily delivered mail addressed to a Ms. Andretta Salinger. Day after day, week in week out, he'd seen the rapid improvement to the property, all the while wondering at the diligence of the new owner, a woman who had almost single-handedly, with only the occasional help of a roofer and a yard worker, brought the Haunted House back from ghostly ruin to a very alive home.

One day with the excuse of delivering a package needing a signature, he left his van by the mail box and approached the barn, where in a T-shirt and jeans the woman had been preparing to paint its wooden double doors. She was surprisingly young and attractive, his own daughter's mid-thirties age and a woman with a vibrant spirit who at the moment was half disguised by paint spattered not only on her clothes but smudged on her face. Dirt as well on her hands and the knees of her jeans evidenced she'd also been gardening. Her shoulder-length natural blond hair was a tangled mess stuck here and there with twigs or bits of leaves from pruning a short section of privet hedge bordering the flagstone walk from the barn to the house as a windbreak.

Typical artist, Spencer said to himself. He'd always thought artists to be different from others, like this young woman seemed to be. And he'd also guessed she might be one from all the mail she received from various museums and art associations. Now he knew he'd guessed right because through one open door of the barn, he could see a painting on an easel and framed canvasses, some partially or fully painted on, some not, leaning against or hanging from the walls.

Hardly an amateur, Spencer thought. Although he knew little about art, the works he saw seemed important somehow, museum or gallery worthy. He handed her the package and then held out his clipboard with a post office form on it. "Afraid I need your signature for this one, Miss."

"Sure," Andretta said, and wiping her hands on her jeans, took the proffered clipboard along with its attached pen and signed next to a prominent *X.*

"Thanks, Miss." Feeling that if he said anything it would be out of place, Spencer just the same couldn't help blurting out, "You sure wrought a miracle here, Ms. Salinger. Old place looks new. And a pleasure to see. Artist, are you?"

"When I find time to be one," the young woman said, and Spencer found himself looking at not just a rather pretty face but one that seemed strongly self-assured and positive, a woman confident in her creativity whose eyes never left his but stared back at him with an unflinching level look.

"Getting there, though," she added, with a sudden and disarming smile. "The house will be all messed up soon, probably. Got a crew coming to fix up my cellar pumps. Flooded to all hell yesterday after that big rain. Same as it did last winter when we got all that snow."

"Yeah, flooding can be a problem. Been there myself. Good luck with it, Miss." And with a "Have a nice day," Spencer headed back to his van.

"You too," Andretta called warmly, and went on painting the barn doors.

Two

The mailman's friendly approval of how she'd improved the looks of the old house lifted Andretta's spirits, which had begun to sag over annoyance with the flooded cellar. *Nice old man,* she thought, and remembered the equally aging real estate agent when she'd first seen the place, and when admitting how badly the place had been, let go: his saying, "Used to be called 'The Haunted House.' Don't know how it got that name. Been selling property here in Connors Falls all my life, and nobody ever died in it that I can recall. Guess kids started naming it that when it begun running down from lack of care."

Andretta had never thought to live any place but in the depths of the big city she'd always called home, especially back in her early teens and starting to show clear signs of developing into an artist. Even before finishing college, she had locally first sold portraits and cityscapes, then had begun experimenting with the abstract, and it wasn't long before wider recognition came with a successful showing of work in a well-recognized gallery.

But Andretta's work hadn't developed much from there. Amidst a long-growing bitterness over money between her parents, her life became far from stable with creativity slowed to a halt by her father's frequent abuse along with his scornfully decrying her moneyless artistic endeavors. And her mother was never there for her, while forever stridently complaining about her own lot in life and blaming everyone else for her own failures. Both made Andretta feel endlessly guilty and unsure.

Family financial crises and the strain of unpaid debts also took its toll on the young artist and were added to by a breakup and failed promises by a boyfriend of several years she'd been crazy about.

Even worse was that instead of pursuing her art when her parents died, first her father, then her mother two years later, Andretta had been obliged to take a hated clerical job in a crowded noisy office just to survive. With that, any confidence in her inner self was slowly eroded and replaced with dark-shadowed unknown fears. Sleepless nights were filled with tormenting unidentified anxieties, daytimes with onslaughts of sudden unexplained crying. Panic

attacks, endless depression, and thoughts of sui-
cide finally sent her to a therapist, a kindly but
no-nonsense older woman.

"It used to be I loved this city," Andretta
had one day blurted, blaming the city for all her
unhappiness, the commuting on the bus and the
subway to work, and the often distant attitudes of
her fellow workers that always seemed unfriend-
liness. "Now I can't stand it. I don't know why.
I just can't. All the never-stop deafening noise,
all the people rushing about with most of them
looking angry, all the big buildings crowding in,
the sky all but shut out. I feel like everything was
crushing me helpless."

But the therapist wisely saw through all
that. She saw another young woman, one who
was the creative artist and on whom the pres-
sures of a different and alien life, so exempli-
fied by all in a big city, had suddenly become
too much. Her quietly patient remark brought
Andretta up short.

"Have you never thought of moving?"

Andretta's immediate angry response: "Moving? Good God, no. Are you kidding? Move?
Move to where? No way. Who needs all that
hassle? Life's bad enough as it is."

A long silence then, in which she alternately
hated and loved the therapist, until finally the
therapist, quietly authoritative, spoke again. "I
want you to do something for me, will you?"

"Like what?" The response a sullen sulk.

"This coming weekend, I'd like you to drive

out of town. Maybe just north on some route for an hour or so until you're well into the country. Drive around and look at things, fields and woods and horses or cows out to pasture: even people too, if you wish. Then write a list of what you saw and tell me about it at our next session."

Looking back, Andretta often wondered if she'd been hypnotized, because she'd done exactly as the woman requested. She'd got in her car on a Sunday morning and had driven away from the city, and once past suburban developments, had found herself in an unfamiliar countryside of small towns, rural farms, and forests. And then, finally, after several hours, had stopped for lunch at a town named Connors Falls, which boasted an old mill where a giant wheel employing the full force of the Connors River was still kept active for tourists, although its role in manufacturing iron tools had long ago ceased.

Looking at a tourist guide folder plucked from a rack in a diner where she'd stopped for lunch, and still wondering why she'd obeyed her therapist and had come there—the town seemed quite ordinary—she'd seen a photo of the Haunted House, among a half dozen others illustrating the attractions of the surrounding countryside. And hadn't given it a thought until she found herself on the narrow country road actually driving past it, and when curious, she'd stopped to look.

When she did, something quite unexpected happened. Perhaps it was the forlorn look of the little stone house set back from the road and nestled against a grove of birch trees that broke an expanse of empty field. Perhaps its abandoned unloved appearance. Perhaps because it was so different from any other house around Connors Falls that it looked so terribly lonely. Perhaps in a way it was how Andretta herself felt, lost and reaching out for help.

Whatever it was, Andretta felt a sudden rush of unexplained emotion, a flood of unleashed feeling she'd never experienced before. She suddenly was again the person she had been, the artist.

She looked and looked at the little house and quite unexpectedly felt something she had not felt for a long time. It was love.

Three

P enny, overly made-up and badly dressed but pretty young woman, answered the phone with a put-on brightness, "Dry Basements, good morning."

One whose inherent fresh sauciness marked her belief that sex ran the world and that she ran sex, she was the all-purpose secretary for the firm she'd announced, which was owned by two brothers, Shawn and Colin Marker. Both in their forties, the two men supported flourishing families by preventing cellars from flooding. Modernizing cellars into usable play rooms or TV rooms was hardly a simple task but a complex one. It often required, besides a knowledge of pumps, an expertise in masonry, drywalling, and lighting, and frequently architectural plans of the basic building structure as well as to adequately understand its foundations. In a sense, they were often building a house within a house.

"Colin, pick up. Ms. Salinger." That was Penny, not very distant across the large relatively bare room that was the office of the two men in Connors Falls, and where the only decoration was a number of large photos of cellars they had brought to a life for a kid's playroom, attractive television viewing, or social gathering.

Colin Marker dutifully obeyed. He was a big brawny man who supported a cropped-short but heavy beard as well as large black rimmed glasses perched on a wide blunt nose and framing bland but intelligent gray eyes. Putting down the pencil with which he'd been making notes on a proposed cellar job, he shoved his glasses up onto his thick graying hair and said, "Yes, Ms. Salinger. Colin Marker." And then, "Yes, I know, but good news finally. And my apologies for not getting to you sooner, but we've finally got you down for tomorrow morning, actually, if that's okay for you. I know it's short notice, but we've had another job cancellation late yesterday." Then, "About eight o'clock, okay? Right. Thank you Ms. Salinger. See you then."

Colin put down the phone and swung around in his chair to address Shawn, seated across the room and studying a large sheet of plans.

"That was the young artist lady at the little stone house on Holway Road. Okay to go ahead. I'll schedule eight o'clock tomorrow for the floor, so you can go ahead and order the pumps. When you looked at the place, you said the ones there were totally rotted out and not worth repairing."

Shawn, quite the opposite from Colin in that he was tall and skinny and balding, said, "Yeah, and when we last talked she agreed to the need for a proper cement floor. Pump's worthless without it, so it means we'll have to dig a lot of dirt first. There's no head room there right now; cellar's damn near crawl space, and we're in for pouring a ton of concrete. At least eight inches deep overall. Bitch of a job, and thank God for the entrance from the outside. Can you imagine if all the dirt had to be lugged in sacks up the stairs into the house first?"

"Don't want to."

Shawn got to work on a to-do list of installing a decent non-flooding cellar in the small stone house on Holway Road, and thus at eight a.m. the following day, Andretta, finishing her first cup of coffee, saw any thought of going to the barn and working on a large half-finished abstract rudely dismissed by the appearance in her driveway of a truck and a van, one with its side emblazoned with the printed words DRY BASEMENTS.

"Holy Jesus," Andretta thought. She was in for at least a week of having life totally disrupted, and so much for peace and quiet and working on the big abstract. Well, she thought, steeling herself somehow to bear with it. In a week or so, palette and brush in hand, she'd be back at it.

Andretta was wrong. She wouldn't resume painting for quite a while.

Four

Besides two classically pretty white clapboarded churches, its historic water mill, and a hospital, Connors Falls, like most towns its size, boasted a police force of thirty-five that included two plainclothes detectives and was presided over by a forty-year veteran, Chief Thomas Walenski.

Long weary of crime of any kind, from homicide to shoplifting, the venerable chief, his head a thatch of prematurely white hair, was by nature a kindly man and hardly a typical cop. He had recently passed retirement age but had stayed on at the request of the mayor and city council because they were hard put to find a replacement with anything like his ability or police record. He had become an institution nobody was anxious to see disappear, someone who still ran a highly efficient police force.

For some time, shaken first by the sudden death of Irma, a much loved autistic child killed by a speeding car, Walenski was then widowed from Estelle, a high school sweetheart to whom he for years had been utterly devoted. Now alone in life except for his work, the venerable police chief had become increasingly tired of seeing minor criminals sent off to jail largely due to his detectives uncovering crimes he thought better punished by rehab and community service. "Heading down a wrong path is hardly corrected by continuing it with a jail sentence," he often said. "Few are bad deep down. They have only gone astray." In his loneliness, the chief had become ever more tolerant of the fate of others.

The day after the brothers Marker had begun work at 24 Holway Road, Walenski, seated at his desk in the crowded police station back of the Town Hall, wearily picked up his landline phone when it rang and said, "Walenski," as though he hated to. After listening for not more than a half minute, he put down the receiver with a muttered, "Christ, now what?" sigh at what he'd heard, and followed with an almost reluctantly issued order to his two detectives, only a few desks away.

"Wake up, you two—911 call they got from Dry Basements. Colin Marker's outfit. They started work at 24 Holway Road and seems they dug up a body. The old haunted house, yeah. Ambulance on its way already. So off you both go. I'll be coming in a few minutes. Best you bring along a uniform with a patrol car. Might have to close the road a while." Leaving the detectives to scramble their departure, the chief phoned the coroner.

"What kind of body? Whose?" That was the always slightly irascible coroner, a middle-aged woman doctor disillusioned with the job.

And Walenski's response: "How the hell do I know, Sally? Haven't seen it yet. Colin Marker dug it up when he went to restore the cellar's dirt floor. But some artist lady's been living there for two years, so it must be pretty far gone, unless she hauled it down and covered it over herself, which can hardly be the case. She's not the type, from what I've heard."

In the little stone house kitchen, Colin Marker gave up rummaging in the refrigerator for a bottle of vodka but found cognac in a close-by cupboard. He poured some in a small glass and took it to his young woman client, who, pale as a sheet, was seated at the kitchen table with Shawn.

"Put this back, Miss," he said, handing Andretta the glass. "Will help steady you down a little. Nasty shock, I'm sure. It was for both me and Shawn when we discovered it. And it's not really a body, ma'am. Just bones. Old ones at that by the look of them. And a big iron bar with them. Can't rise up and harm anybody."

Andretta managed a wan smile, and took the proffered glass of cognac. Being told a few minutes earlier by her cellar contractors that there were the rotting bones of a someone once buried in her cellar had upended everything. It wasn't fear she felt but her refuge in the little stone house destroyed and herself in limbo, no longer immersed in her creations, and the house a welcomed mooring against all the dangerous tides of life, a place of safety. She was only barely aware of both the men who had come yesterday as polite workmen to keep her cellar from flooding, and now were men whom she found herself seeing no longer as people she didn't know but suddenly totally familiar and providing a much needed sense of safety.

The raw essence of the cognac had hardly jarred her halfway back to her senses when she heard the sound of a siren on the road outside, then next the crunch of gravel made by a car in her driveway, and then two other men in her kitchen, complete strangers who said only, "Police. Where is it?" and nothing else except, "Stay right where you are. Nobody leaves here," before disappearing down into the darkness of the cellar through a door in the hall.

Andretta was instantly affronted by their appearance and abrupt order. *Hey, hold on,* was suddenly her thought. *This is my house. Who the hell do you think you are?*

But she didn't have time to dwell on the two men further. Almost immediately there were more men's voices at her front door, and a low-pitched woman's as the house was entered by the coroner, whose greeting was barely a nod before she too went down into the cellar.

Feeling a prisoner in her own home, Andretta could do nothing but stand around as an idle spectator while the invasion of police sought to give an identity to someone long dead in her house who had become rotting bones in the cellar.

Doing so, she began to pull herself together, get over her initial shock, and because it was impossible not to, to take an interest in the comings and goings of the various strangers who had taken possession of not just her home but pretty much her life also.

She had found an ideal observation post at a bench she had long ago placed in front of the house that separated two very large decorative stone flowerpots she'd bought at a country auction soon after she'd moved in. She was seated there when an older man, his hair a thatch of white, came and plunked down on the bench beside her and said, without any preliminaries, "Chief Walenski, Ms. Salinger. How are you coping? Total distraction from everything, especially work, I'm sure."

Walenski had immediately dismissed any thought of her responsibility for the bones inadvertently discovered in her cellar. First basic evidence was that the bones had been under the cellar's dirt floor for years before she had bought the place. He saw only a shaken young woman, and all his instincts went to protecting rather than accusing her.

Andretta was pleasantly surprised by the friendly tone in the elderly man's voice, so different from the bullying "Nobody moves" of the two detectives when they had first burst into the kitchen while she was still cognac-regaining her senses.

"I'm recovering," she said and managed a smile.

"Good," the elderly police officer said, while rested a big hand on her arm in a reassuring way. "But it would be more than understandable if you wanted to sleep or even work somewhere else for a while. There's two good hotels in town. I'm sure the city council would pay for your stay in one a while if I twist arms a little."

Andretta could hardly believe what she was hearing. Few people before she'd bought and moved into her little stone house in Connors Falls had ever spoken to her in such a friendly way. And this was a policeman? She managed somehow to find words to say thank you, and it was almost the last she saw of the police chief, who had turned investigating over to his detectives, although his kind words triggered some of the same emotional response in her that she'd felt on first seeing the house.

This time, however, it wasn't love, it was defiance. She wasn't going to be run out of her home by any murdered person, either by their long-dead bones or by their ghost if there was such a thing. She was going to go right on sleeping in the bedroom upstairs, watching television or reading at night until she fell asleep, and painting during the day in the barn.

It was a determination that was to be sorely tested in the coming days that were filled with the same two miserable detectives who, contrary to the police chief's clear statement of her obvious innocence, seemed to go out of their way to treat her like she had personally murdered the soul who was buried under her cellar dirt. She found infuriating their stream of orders, "Don't touch this," "Don't touch that," when it was her house in which she could damn well do as she wished.

Worse was their forcing her to go with them to the police station for an "interview." Their questioning had gone on and on and still nagged her awake at night.

"Ms. Salinger, we need your help in determining who the bones belong to. You are not under arrest, but you are entitled to have your lawyer present if you wish."

"My lawyer? Good God, no. I have no lawyer. What on earth is this all about?"

"Do you have any idea who the deceased might have been?"

"No."

"Or the rusty iron bar we found with the bones."

"Iron bar? Look, I've only been in my house two years. Ask the real estate guy who sold it to me."

"The previous owner was a Quincy Mortison.

How long did you know him?"

"I never met him. He's long dead. I bought the place from his estate."

"You bought the house furnished. What did you do with all the furniture he left behind?"

"I threw most of it out."

"We're interested in his personal effects."

"Didn't see any."

"There was nothing around to tell you about his life, his friends, his family?"

"Nothing."

It had only stopped when she began wishing she had asked for a lawyer. Not getting a single answer that could help them, they had finally given up and driven her home.

A return to peace lasted barely an hour. The two detectives were soon joined by a positive crowd of other strangers, men in hooded white clothes with big black letters saying FORENSIC who tested for DNA everywhere—in the barn, on all her paintings, and on her, her clothes, on her kitchen utensils and furniture, on stair rails to the cellar, and above all the dirt of the cellar floor, and the bones which lay partially exposed.

And finally prints. Dusting for them never seemed to stop, until one day it finally did. The strange men everywhere were suddenly gone, and silence fell over the house and barn.

It was all over, Andretta thought. Finally. Except it wasn't. Not by a long shot.

Five

One aspect of Police Chief Walenski's character that had caused the city council and mayor to keep him on the job for as long as they could was Walenski's bulldog determination in bringing nearly every case possible to a successful conclusion rather than filing what seemed a dead end as yet another cold case. Boxes in the police station basement archives marked CC were nearly all empty.

Realizing that neither his two detectives nor the coroner could handle any serious investigation of the bones—whose were they, how had their body died, and if homicide, by whom—Walenski dismissed any serious help from the coroner or the aging and useless pathologist at the city morgue. The chief ordered the bones left untouched in their cellar final resting place, consulted his files, and put in a phone call to the prestigious private Liberty Forensic Laboratory, located on spacious grounds not far out of Connors Falls.

If you are a forensic anthropology pathologist, more often than not you have about you an air of scholarly superiority. It comes from the highly scientific skill and knowledge that goes with the job of discovering the identity and social connections, when both are unknown, of one long dead, and often produces not so much a somewhat look of disdain for those you regard as lesser beings, but actual contempt for them.

One such highly specialized pathologist was Derrick Arbiter, who had little time for normal people no matter whom and whose only thoughts ever were the work he was doing with all the various technical and scientific aspect of whatever the work involved.

A leading investigator at Liberty where anthropologic pathology was concerned, this was the person Andretta found brought to her doorstep by Chief Walenski the morning of her second day of freedom from strange men all over the place, with their noise and probing about while she was having a second early morning coffee.

"I need to borrow you, Dr. Arbiter, if that's possible," Walenski had said after he had successfully reached Arbiter by phone and had first duly identified himself and his Connors Falls police force, and then explained his having on his hands a possible homicide of an unknown person.

"Just bones, you say?"

"Old ones," Walenski replied. "A whole skeleton load."

"What kind or bones?" Arbiter came back with. "I presume human. But male? Female? Black, Caucasian, Asian, Aborigine?"

Walenski said he had no idea, and told Arbiter that the bones, a rusty iron bar with them, were buried a mere half foot deep under the dirt floor of a cellar and were apparently a complete skeleton. "They would seem to indicate a homicide," he added.

"On my way," Arbiter said. "Don't touch them."

The brief conversation brought the pathologist to the little stone house at 24 Holway Road, where he met Walenski and also met Andretta Salinger with an uncalled-for remark after a brief introduction that identified him and the reason for his appearance: "Been sleeping with the dead, have you?" he said, with a sardonic and unwitting professional laugh.

It didn't go well with Andretta, whose response was an icy silence. She'd had enough of the unwanted horror of bones, once a decomposing dead body and some live person before dying, to say nothing of police all over the place and herself brought into the police station, the memory of which she could not forget.

Arbiter making light of death in her cellar was close to a last straw in disrupting the peace and quiet she'd experienced during the two years she'd lived in the little stone house. Selling her parents' home had paid for a new furnace, a bathroom with a stall shower, and a new functional kitchen, and the beauty of the surrounding countryside, it's silence and lack of chaos, confusion, and angry city people, had buoyed her artistic talent. The barn had proved a perfect studio for painting, at least in the summer. And to her surprise, she had to grudgingly admit to herself, that she liked the town of Connors Falls. Everything she needed was as easily obtainable as in the metropolis she'd fled as well as much of the same culture: a thriving summer stock theater, a museum, and several first-rate restaurants. All that along with a solid sense of community.

Meanwhile, the contractor, Colin Marker and his brother Shawn, were waiting impatiently to begin building her a whole new cellar which would, she thought, effectively hide any memory of the bones discovered buried there.

The unwanted pathologist newcomer wore a forensic white jumpsuit and had arrived with a similarly white-suited and silent assistant in a van that looked like the coroner's but with LIBERTY FORENSIC LABORATORY in large letters on its side. When introduced by Walenski, Andretta was pointedly sharp.

"Confine yourself to the cellar," she said. "This isn't a rail or bus station; it's a home. And I find anyone using my bathroom there will be hell to pay."

And to Walenski, when Arbiter and his forensic aid had retreated to the cellar, she said,

"How long is this creep staying here? I've got a contractor hanging fire to rebuild the entire cellar."

Walenski could only say with a weak smile, "As long as it takes, Ms. Salinger," while hoping for the best.

Six

The venerable police chief's remark signaled the beginning of an of an uneasy relationship between the intensely emotional artist owner of 24 Holway Road and the disdainful anthropology pathologist who appeared utterly oblivious to anything but his examination of the bones discovered in the cellar.

Andretta had hardly finished listing for Walenski all her household rules for any strangers entering her house when Arbiter reappeared, first to stand silently while she ground coffee beans preparatory to making coffee for herself and the police chief, and then to abruptly and matter-of-factly announce solely to Walenski, as Andretta got down mugs, that the bones in her cellar "were beautiful, and unquestionably belonged to someone who had died some time ago, almost assuredly beaten to death with the iron bar found lying amidst them.

"My first observation," Arbiter said, "will almost certainly be borne out once I we get the bones back to the lab."

It was Walenski who, slightly embarrassed by the pathologist's ignoring Andretta, got him down a mug and poured coffee into it while saying as he did, "You are confirming that we indeed have a homicide on our hands? And that the bones are male, you think?"

"Oh, most definitely," Arbiter said, still ignoring Andretta. "Fellow has marks all over him that say a violent end. Fibula and tibia bruising. Defending himself, I presume. It was the one bash on his occipital that ended him, although possibly he also died from strangulation. I noticed disturbance around his third cervical at the base of the mandible as well as a definite crack on the transverse of his upper hyoid."

"How long have the bones been down there?" Walenski asked, confused by Arbiter's scientific deductions.

"More than a hundred years, I think," Arbiter replied. "At first glance it would seem he was buried very soon after he met his fate."

The complete casualness of the pathologist's explanation was almost too much for the curiosity his words ignited in Andretta, although she was immediately more appalled by the time the bones had lain in her cellar than she was by evidence of homicide. The pathologist's invasion of her home momentarily forgotten, she burst out with, "More than a hundred years? How can you tell that?"

Arbiter appeared to recognize her presence for the first time before responding. "Oh, it's quite obvious. Bones are finger-pointers as to why they have come to be so. The state of deterioration of the bones themselves tells a story. I'll know more at the lab after carbon-14 testing, X-rays, and all that sort of thing."

Further talk was interrupted by the appearance of Arbiter's assistant, who came up out of the cellar with a rusty iron bar, some dirt still clinging to it, and two large plastic bags, one filled to bulging with jumbled-about bones, the other protecting the long-buried skull.

"Put them right there," Arbiter said, pointing to the kitchen table as though he owned it, and when the bones were duly placed, he added, not without an air of pride, "Lovely lot. Male, Caucasian, about five-foot-six, I'd guess, relatively young and underweight."

Andretta slowly raised her eyes from staring at the skull that seemed all teeth and grinning back at her and finally found her voice. "Do they have to be on my kitchen table?"

"No, I don't suppose so. I'll have them off to the lab right now." The pathologist, obviously amused at her distress, called out to his assistant, who had disappeared briefly and was just reappearing with a sack of dirt from the cellar.

"Why the dirt?" Walenski asked.

"It could possibly explain any time gap

between the skeleton's death and its burial. Not particularly important I should imagine. Just rounds out a picture."

With Andretta, although superficially mollified by the police chief's authoritative although usual friendly presence, it wasn't so easy. While realizing that she was probably stuck with the anthropology pathologist for a while, at least, his being in her kitchen was still too much, and she was hardly happy about it. She maintained a grudging and silent assent, however, while managing nothing more than a brief glance at him.

"So now what's your next step, Dr. Arbiter?" Walenski said, still embarrassed by Arbiter's rudeness, and keeping up his peacemaking attitude as the pathologist gestured to the lab assistant to take the bones and skull away.

"My next step is to get these lovely bones spread out on a slab," Arbiter said, "and more accurately ascertain the exact date and the how of his demise. When I'm done with a lab investigation, Chief, it's then back to you," he added condescendingly. "Who he was and who killed him is mostly in your hands. I'm afraid you are going to have to investigate the world back in the eighteen hundreds to find both the ownership of the bones as well as the identity of their killer. Good luck with it." And then, almost with an amused sneer, "If nobody else, I'm sure the lady here would like to know who she's been living with."

"I'm sure she would," the police chief said, "if

for no other reason than to arm herself against the media who forever, as their want, will look to her for answers. Am I right, Ms. Salinger?"

Andretta tried to find a response and couldn't. Through the mist of her dislike of the pathologist, she suddenly had a vague feeling that she was involved, like it or not, in the police investigation of the unwanted death in her cellar, and realized there was probably no way to avoid it. What about her work, then? What about the peaceful life she had found far from the once loved and now hated big city? It seemed hopelessly gone, and she felt more than ever isolated from all she'd found living in the little stone house whose once title of "haunted" now seemed so appropriate.

Seven

S he didn't have to wait long to hear from the police chief, perhaps only a week, during which she forced herself to work and to ignore any police activities. She was in the barn mid-morning when her cell phone rang, interrupting a difficult color blend in the big abstract on her easel she had resumed working on.

"Derrick Arbiter is ready for us," Chief Walenski said. "I'm sure you'll want to know what he'll have to say in his investigations of the bones. We'll be off to the morgue as soon as you are ready."

Andretta knew she had to go if for no other reason than to please the police chief, who had been so kind and considerate, and so, within an hour, she found herself in a police car with him, an unwilling visitor to the morgue at Liberty Laboratory. Not knowing quite what to expect, she found it a brightly lit busy place in a suburban modern glass building that seemed a collection of electronics and busy technicians all assembled into more of a large abstract painting of swirling forms and colors than what was essentially a place of death.

She and the police chief were greeted by the anthropology pathologist, who seemed utterly unconcerned by the constant disembodiments of the unfeeling dead that were his life.

"Got him all ready to greet you," he said, with an almost good cheer that Andretta instantly found irritating, and she unwillingly followed the pathologist and the police chief past several raised slab horrifyingly occupied by naked once alive women being dissected by lab technicians and another pathologist.

"Did X-rays and carbon-14 testing affirm your first conclusions about time and method of death?" she heard Walenski ask.

"Oh, indeed. And to the very month. Mid- to late summer would be almost certain. August or September. And most definitely of the year 1868."

Derrick Arbiter, laughing with the pleasure of it all, led a weaving path through the big laboratory room to a gurney where Andretta, avoiding even a glance at a nearby corpse, saw carefully spread out, in clear full form, the now clean iron bar next to them, and as though living, except they were a once person's skeleton, the bones of someone who for one hundred and fifty years, according now to the anthropologist, had resided in her cellar.

"There you have him," Arbiter said. "Bashed about a bit with the iron bar. Head wound definitely. Bar just fits the crushed-in bone of the skull, and he was definitely also strangled."

"Bashed about how?" Walenski demanded, the police chief undeterred by the nearby very naked corpse of an elderly woman. He at once sensed a possible clue in the homicide and got out his notebook and a pencil stub.

"Heavy blows here," Arbiter responded, pointing to the lower leg of the laid-out skeleton. "Here where there's cracks, and then here." He pointed out a spot on the femur. "Here on the lower brachium. All these areas of bruises, still visible after all these years, indicate he was defending himself from blows. Bones reveal what happened in life's last few moments long after the flesh is gone. It's the ones on this one's skull, here first on the sphenoid up front and then the big blow to the posterior cranial that finished him off."

Looking at the grimacing skull, Andretta felt a chill run through her whole body as though she herself had been beaten then killed. She heard Arbiter say, "We've got a face to replace the skull if you'd like to look. It's not a perfect likeness but pretty close." He called out, "Elena!"

A slightly robust young woman in a long chemical-stained smock appeared, and when confronted by strangers, vaguely tried to rearrange hair that was in complete disarray. "Sir?"

"Elena, kindly show our guests the picture you composed last night of the deceased."

"My pleasure, sir," and Andretta and Walenski were ushered away from the bones to an enclosed space where there was a large-scale screen on a wall above a crowded desk with a computer keyboard and two smaller monitors, one with a picture of the skull she'd just seen on the gurney along with the a carefully arranged pattern of bones.

Unable not to, Andretta found herself, while not understanding a single word, listening to a lengthy technical explanation of how and why various aspects of the skull slowly went through a developing series of pictures, which she saw on the big screen, one after another, to become the characterless computer face of a young clean-shaven man.

"There you are," Arbiter declared proudly. "Elena's wizardry. A mug shot of our victim who's been buried for so long under your cellar floor, Ms. Salinger."

Andretta felt it hard to speak. She stared at the bleak expressionless face. The face stared back at her, lifelessly, its very silence saying, "Yes, look at me. I've been sharing your house for all the time you've been living in it. I've been right there with you while you slept."

She heard Walenski utter words of astonishment and praise, and Arbiter say in a know-it-all tone that the only way to determine the person's identity so long ago was to work backwards, perhaps through property ownership.

"All yours, Chief," Arbiter added condescendingly. "But that's not exactly my field of expertise."

And so, there it was, a face but no name, the face of a good-looking young man instead of just a skull. But it didn't really help. Who did both belong to all those far-off years in centuries past? Who was he? How and why had he died?

Taking leave of the pathologist and on the way back to town, she and Walenski were both silent, Andretta seeing herself in Civil War days when the smoke and thunder of cannon and the dying cries of bayonet-wielding soldiers was the norm.

Until she suddenly heard Walenski say, "Golly, what a lulu. A face for sure but no identity of any kind. Not just who was he, but why he was there, and why was he murdered in the first place, and by whom. Looks like there will be a need to ferret about a lot in history. I'd put my detectives to work on it, but they have an important fraud case against a city councilman that has to take precedence. So it looks like I'll have to do their work for them. And for a start, when I can get to it, as Arbiter suggested, work backwards from the person who sold you your house until we find who built it, and more importantly, who was living in it around 1868."

Hearing the tired resignation in his voice,

Andretta glanced at him. The police chief looked worn out. *Getting too old for the job*, she thought, and felt an odd and unexpected concern for him. Why should he have to tackle such a job at his age? It didn't seem fair. Those two bloody worthless detectives, shame on them.

And then in another long silence between them, she again felt a disturbing something else she'd felt before. She had a sense she owed Walenski one. Hadn't he been kindness itself in protecting her when he could from the chaos of investigation that had filled her home? He had been a wall between her and his detectives and the forensic squad. "Here, you. Mind your manners. Speak politely to the lady. This is her home, not a lock up." And, "Keep your voices down and stop shouting." And, "Drag mud into the house and you'll clean it up."

She knew then, without thinking further, that she ought to help out wherever possible. After all, like it or not, she was involved in a homicide that had occurred in her house, not in somebody else's. And it was her life that had been disrupted. So, right now, for a start, there was no reason to wait for Walenski or anybody else to spend time discovering who was the original owner of her little stone house and helping to bring an end to the whole police investigation. As the pathologist Arbiter had suggested, she was quite capable, she felt sure, of finding that out herself, and she decided impulsively to at least give a try at helping to get things back to normal.

In the odd chance that the real estate agent who'd sold her the house might have a record of past ownership, she decided to see him. He'd represented the property for the estate of someone named Quincy Mortison, and momentarily putting aside thoughts of the painting she wanted to get back to, she went to his office at Connors Falls.

Eight

Andretta found the friendly agent who had sold her the house to have retired and been replaced by a rather prissy young man, with a receding hairline and equally thin wispy mustache, and who was one of those people who felt that once a property had either been sold or bought that any further work involved was something to be avoided at any cost. Just getting the name and address of the owner previous to the Quincy Mortison estate was like extracting teeth that didn't want extracting, with wispy mustache a hundred percent reluctant to reveal anything.

"You must have their name on the title of the house you received on purchase." That was agent wispy mustache.

"I don't," Andretta shot back. "I only have the name of the man who sold me the house.

Quincy Mortison. I mean his estate. I'm asking for the name of whomever he bought it from."

"You don't have it?" Behind the mustache was a maddening smirk, "Oh, dear. I have so many purchases and sales on the books. I'll have to look it up."

"Please do."

"Er, yes. Of course."

"Now."

And then a long wait as the agent needlessly shuffled around papers on his cluttered desk until he finally decided that shuffling through his memory was easier. "Ah, yes. Prior owners. Yes, indeed."

And again, a silence while he simply stared at Andretta, who, thoroughly exasperated, said, "Well?"

Again an "Ah, yes." And then finally bursting out with, "Mortison. Yes, I suppose Ephram Mortison."

"Address?"

"Address? Ah, yes, address." Followed by more shuffled papers. "Number 24 Holway Road."

Andretta tried hard not to laugh, and it was not without a frustrated sigh of relief that she finally fled the man's office when wispy mustache could provide no farther-back owner than someone also named Mortison, who had the odd biblical first name of Ephram, as well as the address of the lawyer who had handled his sale to Quincy Mortison.

In for a penny, she thought, and the next

stop was the Connors Falls law office of Terrance, Reilly and Lee, none of whom were, not surprisingly, available for such casual questioning about the present and past of one of their clients. Such information was delegated to a junior associate who, when Andretta visited the firm, proved to be an overweight, pale, nervous, and sloppily dressed young man by the name of Davis Lacey, who nevertheless rose to the occasion and, perhaps to show off his importance as a legal gopher, was eagerly helpful. And further to Andretta's surprise, a source of much wanted information as well.

"Quincy Mortison, indeed, yes," young Lacey offered. "The last, I believe, in a long line of Mortisons. He came right after Ephram, who died in 1910."

"You said 'line,'" Andretta quickly interjected. "Do you know of other Mortisons?"

Lacey virtually beamed with pride at the information he could provide. "Oh, I know all the Mortisons, starting in 1850-something with Alquist, the billionaire railroad baron who, incidentally, built your cottage, Ms. Salinger. Back around 1859, I believe. He was born in 1800, died in 1866, and was followed by Axel and then Ezra, Jessup, and Noah before Ephram and Quincy."

His so confidently reeling off the biblical names of the long dead over nearly two centuries almost overwhelmed Andretta with surprise. "You said railroad?" she demanded.

"Yes, indeed. The early Mortisons were

railroading tycoons. They started with owning the Great Lakes and Northern. That was one of the first rail lines west of the Mississippi. Alquist's son Axel took it over on Alquist's death. And Ezra inherited it after Axel was gone, but before he went, had first sold Great Lakes to buy the Northwestern and Idaho, which then, much later, around 1915, became the line we know today as the Union Pacific. Jessup ran that one. He was a hoot. Thought being a Mortison was next to God, and commissioned some writer to pen a biog of the family.

"Alquist," Lacey couldn't help giggling, his whole overweight frame positively jiggling with delight, and lowering his voice to an almost conspiratorial whisper, "built 24 Holway for a mistress, apparently. A famous French cabaret actress. Such scandal in those days. His proper wife, Barbara, came from a socially prominent family in, I believe, Boston."

Andretta, still coming to grips with such an avalanche of information, and trying to write down all she heard, finally asked, "How is it you know so much about railroads?"

"Oh, I don't, really. Dreadful things. I'd almost rather walk than ride in one. *Choo-choo-choo* and *The Wabash Cannonball* and all that sort of thing was never for me. But my father had a book on the early railroad acquisitions of the Mortison family. It was the only book in our house, so I read a lot of it because there was nothing else to read."

Andretta suddenly had a brief memory of a big locomotive hurtling at her from a jumble of long-faded daguerreotype photos of old-fashioned railroad trains, news clippings, and people in the little framed collage hanging unobtrusively in her kitchen. It was the only thing she hadn't thrown out when she'd moved in to completely redo the place. She had always respected collages as serious works of art and had kept this one, seeing it not only as first rate, but out of respect for its unknown creator. Whoever that was, the he or she who had signed the work only with the letter *M*, they had shown the most exhaustive attention to detail, right down to a tongue of bright flame leaping from the engineer platform of the giant locomotive dominating the collage as coal or wood was fed into its huge boiler and a cloud of black smoke billowed upward from its tall funnel. "It says 'Hello' to me," Andretta would always say to any who asked why she'd kept it.

Police Chief Walenski's two detectives had never bothered with the collage other than wiping it for a routine DNA, thinking, as did Andretta, that it could hardly have had anything to do with the bones of someone buried in her cellar.

She and they were wrong.

Nine

"Your little stone house built by a famous early railroad baron, the kind one reads about in history books? Can you believe it, Ms. Salinger?" Chief Walenski said. "Well done, young lady. Puts both me and my detectives to shame."

Andretta, seated with coffee with the police chief, had just told him what she had learned from Davis Lacey at the law firm of Terrance, Reilly and Lee. Sunlight pouring through the window of Walenski's cramped office seemed a sharp contrast to what Andretta had learned of Alquist buying and selling railroads as he ensconced a mistress in her house. It seemed not just another time but a whole other world of power.

Railroads meant Chinese immigrant laborers back then, laying tracks for giant coal-burning steam locomotives pulling rickety wooden cars and meeting each other head-to-head on the single line finally completed from the East Coast to the West. There at such a major success, the trains were greeted by a crowd of men wearing pearl-gray waistcoats and the dangling chains of gold watches and doffing top hats at each other. The imagery just didn't fit either with the large abstract paintings she was doing in the barn of the little stone house. Or with all the bustling police activity around Walenski's office.

"And meanwhile, keep it up, if you feel like it," Walenski continued, refreshing both their coffees. He laughed lightly. "Looks like I might have to deputize you."

But Andretta, who felt a glow of enjoyment at the success she'd had, found herself saying, "You'll do no such thing," surprising even herself at the thought. "Let's see what more I can find on my own."

But even as she spoke, she didn't really want to go on playing detective, the only term she could think of that applied to what she had just done. At the same time, she wasn't able to think about giving it up either. When reluctantly she left the police chief with his thanks, Andretta, for all her impulsive bravado, and as she drove away from the police station and left Connors Falls behind, realized she had to face facts.

Okay to say she could get on with it, but what next? She had no constructive idea. The police chief, become busy with something else, hadn't suggested anything, and so it was with great reluctance that she decided to ask for help in getting started from the only person she knew, other than Walenski, who was familiar with the homicide discovered in her cellar.

Accordingly, and a day later, the anthropology pathologist Dr. Derrick Arbiter wasn't at all happy when, while dissecting a corpse at the prestigious Liberty Forensics Laboratory, he was told there was a lady at the reception desk who would like to see him.

"A lady? What lady? Who is she?" Derrick Arbiter had no girlfriend nor socialized much anywhere with any group that might have provided him with one.

"I have no idea, sir. She said you'd worked on a homicide at her house."

Time for a brief moment stood still in Arbiter. "Damn it," he muttered, in a tone that was half curiosity at the idea of any lady daring to come to see him without an appointment, and half annoyance at exactly who this lady had to be. He drew a resigned breath and said, "Show her in," which was a statement that slipped out of him inadvertently, when he actually meant to say, "Tell her I'm not here."

Such was his standing at the Liberty Laboratory that Andretta, escorted by a breathless and obsequious receptionist, appeared in almost no time in the pathology area with its naked half-dissected bodies and pungent odor of death and chemicals to find Arbiter in working scrubs and tinkering with the unidentifiable half-mummified remains of an elderly woman.

The haughty pathologist's manner was professionally cool and unflustered as though her appearance in his lab was perfectly normal. "Yes? It's Ms. Salinger, is it? What can I do for you?" He put out a rather bloodstained rubber gloved hand to be shaken. Andretta ignored it.

She had steeled herself for the meeting, and managing to hide her disdain of the pathologist, told him that Chief Walenski had suggested she see if he had any ideas how to proceed in her search for further information on the original owner of her home.

Her abruptness and assumed air of self-assurance that she didn't at all feel took Arbiter off-balance, and after sputtering a moment rather indignantly, he managed to ask her what he could do and how far she'd already got in her search.

Told of Alquist's notable fame as a billionaire railroad baron, he was unable not to show interest. Such a totally unexpected fact gave quite a new dimension in his mind to the bones he had investigated. Various visions of life around the time of the Civil War at once rose in his mind: venerable bearded men posing grandly for portraits in the dress clothes fashionable at the time, steaming locomotives, ladies in billowing skirts and laced in bodices, and, of course, men in gray, bayonets flashing, as they marched to their death in the Civil War conflict against marching men in blue from the north.

"A railroad baron?" Arbiter said, unable not

to speak with reasonable civility. "One of those, was he?" And in spite of himself, "How very interesting. But why on earth would you wish to know more about him?" Without his realizing it, Arbiter was hooked.

Andretta had unwittingly struck a chord. The railroad and then later the oil barons in history had always excited Arbiter's curiosity, mostly due to their being a law unto themselves, which the anthropologist thought was a basic in scientific discovery.

Andretta, unaware of the reason for his sudden interest, gained courage from his becoming positive. "He built my little stone house," she said, "where you found the bones, and it may even have been occupied by his son Axel about the same time you told us the person whose bones you examined was buried in the cellar."

"You feel there's a connection between the bones and the railroad baron?"

"Not the baron, but his son," Andretta replied. "And whether there is or isn't, Chief Walenski says the bones you examined are a homicide that has to be investigated, and that an investigation has to start with knowing something of the historical time in which they were placed there. Would you have any ideas as to where to start? The police chief is tied down for the moment on a big fraud case."

A little surprised by Andretta's seeming close connection to the police chief and her apparent progress in investigating the homicide, Arbiter began to see her in a different light, perhaps someone he should not be so quick to look down upon. For the moment, however, all he could first manage was "Hmm," but then the anthropologist in him overtook the pathologist, and he mentally tried to organize all the various steps there might be where he was concerned in the case the police sought to solve. Besides anthropologically interesting socially, it was important to him and his work to continue a close liaison with the Connors Falls police, who brought a lot of business to the lab that their own pathologist or the coroner couldn't handle, and he'd long maintained a close grudging relationship with Chief Walenski.

"Well," he said after what seemed to Andretta an interminably long silence, "You could start with newspaper reports of the times, if any have been kept. A figure such as one of those legendary railroad barons would surely have captured headlines. I should think perhaps a visit to the regional newspaper, *The Weekly Echo*. They have been in business forever, I believe, and could perhaps have archived some of their headlines of the time."

There was a silence. Andretta waited for more, which finally came with Arbiter rather awkwardly saying, "Yes, *The Weekly Echo*. We know the editor, who has been helpful to the lab, and I'll come with you, if you like."

Oh, God, no, she thought.

Ten

But it was, "Oh, God, yes."

"The *Echo*?" Andretta demanded. The pathologist's suggestion caught her by surprise. She knew *The Weekly Echo* well, if only for its classified ads and "Food of the Week" bargains run by the supermarket she patronized. Arbiter had perhaps come up with a good idea, to see what they might have on life back in the 1860s and 1870s, but the thought of his tying himself to a visit made her wish she'd never come to see him, let alone ask for his help.

"Just a chance shot," Arbiter said, offering her a rather meaningless smile.

Unable to find a valid reason for not agreeing, Andretta soon found herself with the overbearing pathologist she disdained headed for the offices of *The Weekly Echo*, which, published in Connors Falls, had a far-reaching readership halfway across the state. It had been in business since before the Civil War, when a local citizen by the name of Joshua Byners had begun sending out newsletters warning of an approaching dangerous dispute over abolition and states' rights between the Southern states and those of the North.

Once again, she felt unreal, no longer the person she was before the discovery of bones in her cellar. Once again, she felt distant from her unfinished big abstract in her barn that she had started in the peace and quiet of the little stone cottage she'd bought that was so far removed from her first life in the uproar of the big city. Was it only last week that she had been awakened by the chatter of birds under the eaves outside her bedroom window where they had chosen to nest, and she'd almost daily seen deer grazing on surrounding fields? And twice now on an evening, a fox. City bred, she'd been awed, and still was, although now trying at the same time to come to grips with someone long ago murdered and buried in her cellar.

Perhaps nothing was a more forcible reminder that she had become thoroughly accustomed to the entirely different manner of living in the countryside than her warm greeting by the newspaper's editor and publisher himself, the affable friendly Henry Bloom, a slight, graying, bespectacled veteran journalist.

"Oh, my goodness, so you're the young artist lady I heard purchased the Haunted House that has sat forlornly unoccupied for so many years. How very nice to meet you."

Won over completely, and her resentment of Arbiter's single-minded insistence he accompany her half forgotten, Andretta found herself escorted through the small crowded newsroom, where reporters crouched over their computer keyboards, to meet the gushy spinster who was in charge of the paper's archives as well as the classifieds.

Her name was Adelaide, and she was a large officious lady, looking to be in her sixties, who wore a flowered yellow dress and was further distinguished by a tight blue-tinted permanent. Bifocal rimless eyeglasses were secured to her by a narrow ribbon and which, when not perched on her long rather dominant nose, dangled down over her expansive bosom. She had been working for *The Weekly Echo* for over forty years, and she proved a treasure.

"Old news article about that dreadful railroad baron Alquist Mortison? Goodness me, yes. I have a fair number of front pages featuring him. They were fortunately kept in dry places by my early-on predecessors before dehumidifiers came along, and then put behind protective glass with the most fragile front pages on digital the moment we computerized. There are quite a few."

Andretta and Arbiter were promptly led to a side room, where there was a computer with a large monitor, and they had hardly been seated when the monitor flickered with light and they saw themselves looking at a faded, barely legible front page of *The Weekly Echo* dated 1870 that announced the results of a council election along with discovery of a mass grave of Confederate troops brought to light by a town decision to dig new wells on areas of expansion.

"Alquist came earlier. Let me see which year," the robust Adelaide said. "Perhaps one headlining that scandalous liaison between Alquist and his mistress."

"Oh?" Arbiter sat up straight. "A mistress?"

"Oh, yes, a dreadful French actress he flaunted quite publicly with no shame whatsoever. Céline Charlette. A most shocking lady. She had no morals at all."

The monitor flashed and promptly produced a *Weekly Echo* front page dated April 23, 1866, and Andretta found herself looking at a headline announcing Alquist Mortison's death, and mentioning along with his railroad ownership his long relationship with the notorious French actress for whom he had built a small stone house outside Connors Falls in 1860.

"Love nest," Adelaide sniffed.

"But how interesting," muttered Arbiter as he eagerly pounced on the front page announcement. "Any mention of a will?"

"Afraid not," Adelaide said, "But I have other front pages with articles about him before he died."

The monitor flashed again and Andretta found herself looking at four front pages dated

1859, 1860, and 1871. Each featured prominent headlines and subheadings in the style of the day. Alquist Mortison's purchase of the Great Lakes and Northern rail line right before the Civil War was headlined in the 1860 paper. Mention of his association with Céline Charlette, along with an article about her fame on the American stage after coming to the country from France, appeared under a headline in an 1861 edition.

"Shocking lady," Adelaide said, her distaste of the actress evident in her every word. "French. What else."

With nothing further to show, and after reading as much of the front pages preserved by the newspaper as time would allow, Andretta and pathologist Derrick Arbiter prepared to take leave of *The Weekly Echo*. Andretta was excited at having learned that her home had been built by one so famous but at the same time disappointed that she hadn't learned anything more directly leading to the why and the how of the bones in her cellar.

"So we know," she said, "that Mortison built my house for his mistress sometime before 1860, and that he died in '66. But so what? Where does that get us?"

"To his will," Arbiter said, ignoring her disappointment and unable to contain a burst of scientific exactness. He rose to his feet, all ready to go, and was thanking the flowery Adelaide when Andretta said, "Wait. Wait."

Her artist's eye had spotted something on

the front page of the 1860 newspaper that the dramatic and overblown headlines had caused both her and Arbiter to miss. "Take a look at this," she said, and pointed to a small column heading that was so faded as to be almost invisible. It read "Women Arrested," and when Arbiter, almost in spite of himself, came back, he bent closely to the front page to read haltingly the small fading letters: "Sheriff Thomas, somebody, can't quite make it out, I think Crawley maybe," and went on to read, "today arrested two women outside a house on Holway Road who were shouting obscenities at the owner, Miss Céline Charlette, and her son. The women were bustled into a van and will appear before a magistrate on charges of disturbing the peace."

Andretta stepped back from the newspaper front page. "So Miss Charlette was living in my house along with a child who had to be her son. Could that child be by anyone other than Alquist Mortison?"

Eleven

"Agreed," the anthropology-steeped pathologist said, his tone almost reluctant because he felt agreeing to zany opinions by any nonscientist to be a humiliating surrender. "But I'm not at all sure where it gets us. We've found the original owner of your house and its occupant, but so what? Neither is a definite clue to the identity of the bones, nor any clue whatsoever as to who was the murderer and why."

Andretta controlled an impulse to snap back with, "I resent your use of the word *we*," but managed to say more tactfully, even though feeling disappointed when she'd somehow hoped for something more definite, "Maybe, but now at least we have some sort of picture of what went on at my house at the very time, according to you and your forensic examination that, the bones were buried there."

"Precisely," Arbiter said as though the thought had been his. And after a moment's rapid recollection, continuing with, "Starting perhaps with that son, if he indeed was Mortison's."

"Of course he was Mortison's. Who else?" Andretta shot back. "Alquist surely would never have tolerated Céline Charlette's son's presence in the house if the child was by anyone other than himself, a man so self-important and concerned with his image."

"Precisely," Arbiter responded, his tone slightly truculent, although seizing the thought as his own. And then, taking the reins in pursuit of who had been murdered and by whom, he brightened and said, "But where does that leave us? A wayward mother with an illegitimate child with no name. Our next step has to be to determine precisely who he was. Fathers back then often gave sons names of someone amidst their ancestry. Names like Absalom, Elon, Asa, Asher, and Abraham, or some very rare ones I remember once running across like Yitzhak and Yahbin and Minot."

"Yahbin? Minot?"

"And Yitzhak, yeah, I know. Odd. But all tribal desert kings, and probably from the earliest biblical history that we read in grad school in a required course on social anthropology. Perhaps we might find an intimation of sorts there."

Andretta hardly heard him. Saying goodbye and thanking Adelaide and Bloom as they walked out, she didn't think that finding a name for Céline Charlette's son was a worthwhile course to follow. No matter what name Arbiter might find, there was no way to justify affixing it to the actress's child.

But what, in this case, she wondered was practical? Completely at odds, she decided to go back to Police Chief Walenski to see if he had any suggestions, and found him in his cluttered office, consulting with one of his detectives along with a uniformed officer, looking into a near fatal traffic accident following a police car chase.

"I think you are probably right," he said to Andretta after he'd seated her with coffee. "Our pathology friend might turn up any number of suitable family names that landed on the child. But without a birth certificate, we're stuck to know which name is the correct one. And finding a birth certificate is more likely than not a total impossibility. Any hospital ceased to exist long ago, if indeed he was born in one and not at home with the assistance of a midwife, which was more often than not the case in those days."

"Maybe," Andretta said, still with the insistent feeling she was on to something, simply because apparently the famous actress had lived in her cottage virtually at the same time someone had been murdered there.

She said, "But perhaps we should be looking among missing persons." She broke off, surprised at her own sudden thought, and a little embarrassed because she had no idea where or how they could find anything about anyone gone missing over a hundred and fifty years ago. In a sudden silence that fell over her and Walenski, Andretta uncomfortably felt the old police chief staring at her.

Walenski broke the silence. "Don't short change yourself, Ms. Salinger. You are on to something, but you need help." And he suddenly thought of a young uniformed officer not yet a detective but one whose brightness and hard work had caused him to take a personal interest in. He seized his telephone and abruptly commanded, "Tell Jamie Smith to come to my office. And on the double."

He hung up and said to Andretta, "Regretfully, I'm too busy at the moment with several other cases to go much further with this one. My detectives also. The officer coming is someone I trust to stand in for me."

He had hardly spoken when there was a knock on his door, the summoned Jamie appeared, and Andretta found herself looking at a young uniformed policewoman with the taut figure of an athlete, a holstered Glock revolver hanging from her police utility belt and longish dark hair that stuck out from behind her baseball cap like a flag.

"Sir," she said.

"Sit," Walenski ordered, and when she did, "Jamie, this is Ms. Salinger, who owns the once haunted house on Holway Road where we found a brace of human bones from a murder around 1868. Our investigation has led us to try to tack an identity to a young man who we believe lived in that cottage at the time. Ms. Salinger will fill you in on the details. Start with our records and keep me posted."

"Yes, sir." And Jamie promptly made Andretta's day when, escorting Andretta from Walenski's office, she said, "I'm a fan of yours, Ms. Salinger. I've seen all your work in the Fusion Gallery, which showed them this spring."

"It's Andretta," Andretta said, hardly believing what she'd heard. Art appreciation from a policewoman?

"Yes, ma'am. Andretta. And I particularly love the one you called *Blue*."

The exchange took away all the frustration Andretta was feeling in her search for the identity of the bones found buried in her cellar, and even before following Jamie to a desk in a room Jamie said was the records section, and while briefly filling Jamie in on what she'd learned so far, she felt hopes rise, and that she was finally getting someplace.

A tall bookshelf packed with files shared space with a desk with a large PC monitor. "Those files," Jamie explained, "are mostly just the past five years, so what we're looking for wouldn't be in any of them. The Chief, God bless him, may seem a little old-fashioned, but we're a modern police force, and most of our back records were digitized about eight years ago. So let's see what we've got for way back, and when? 1868? Missing person files would come up only in fifty-year groups. Not that many people go missing."

Sitting down after pulling up chairs for herself and Andretta, the young police officer went to work on the computer keyboard. Images, words, numbers flashed on the monitor until it suddenly showed a list of about a hundred names. "It averages only about one person a year, if that," Jamie said. "So we'll need to see anyone possibly with what name—Mortison? Or perhaps Charlette?"

She went to work, and two columns of names appeared with dates besides them. She blocked off those dated from 1860 to 1870. There were only six, one in 1861 and five during the years 1866 to 1870, with none shown during the years 1862 through 1865. "Probably scores missing those years," Jamie said, "but records weren't kept during the Civil War."

Andretta looked at the five 1866 to 1870 names. They were Boyd Spring, Mary Townsend, Sadie Burke, and Agnes Smith. The fifth had only one identifying name, Minot.

"Any of those?" Jamie asked. "Not many, and I'm afraid no Mortison or Charlette."

Andretta hardly heard her. Hadn't Arbiter mentioned the name Minot, along with the names of some other very early desert kings? At the same time, something deep in her memory jarred. The wonderfully creative collage of old railroad trains she'd kept hanging in the kitchen out of respect for the unknown artist. It had been signed with only the letter *M*.

Could the bones in her cellar belong to some missing person named Minot, who was the presumed artist of her wonderful railroad collage, as well as quite possibly the child of the railroad baron Alquist?

Twelve

"Looks like they more than likely are," Chief Walenski said when Andretta and Jamie reported their findings. "DNA testing showed the bones matched some of the DNA on your collage of railroading the way it was way back then. But it doesn't tell us this Minot's family name, if indeed it was either Charlette or Mortison. We are still only supposing, and I can't solve a homicide on supposition. We need cold hard facts as evidence, and that means positive proof of who the devil Minot *was*."

"Arbiter said the bones belonged to someone age twenty," Andretta reminded him, "which again points a finger at the Minot who Jamie found missing."

"Hmm. Fits. So we can proceed on the presumption that your collage artist is actually our victim," Walenski said, "if DNA confirms it, but that still doesn't tell us factually who he was, nor who he was murdered by, or why."

He had found a free moment to come by Andretta's little stone house to discuss what she had discovered with police officer Jamie in digitized records and to see for himself the little collage again. The weather was warm. He, Andretta, and Jamie, who had driven Walenski out in a police car, sat on the bench between the big stone flowerpots with some iced tea Andretta had mixed up.

"But," the venerable old officer went on, "In homicides, and even though you must be governed by cold hard facts, you often also have to listen to intuition or hunches to get to the truth, if you will, that, no matter how far-fetched, can more often than not lead you to those facts. In our case that means deciding to go with Minot being our bones, and if so, at the same time, possibly being connected with the Mortisons, and that connection our belief in his being the child of Miss Céline Charlette, and thus a half-brother of Axel."

Andretta agreed and said, "So what's our next step, then?" She kept to herself that she felt badly that the bones in her cellar belonged to the talented artist who had created her little railroad collage.

"A look at the life back then of Alquist Mortison, for a start," the chief said. "First target: Alquist and his son Axel, who was second to own the Great Lakes and Northern Railroad, before he sold it to Northwestern and Idaho. Both were all over your house, so who were these guys privately? You've already seen their news headlines, but when I say privately, I mean just that. Other than news headlines, what's been said about them? Surely someone must have written a book about Alquist."

Jamie said, "I can research that on the Harvard online library, or even The Library of Congress."

Andretta said, "I'll try Yale and the big public library in New York."

Both she and Jamie got to work at once on their laptops, and books proved to be a strong lead. Andretta soon found one in the digital stacks at Yale, where Alquist had been a student. Written by a J. Arthur Herman, it mostly extolled the nefarious railroad takeovers and deals Alquist had made on his way to ownership of the Great Lakes and Northern, but offered disappointingly little of his personal life. It did not even mention his liaison with Céline Charlette. All Andretta was able to gather was that he was a ruthlessly cruel man who once had two Chinese laborers tied down on railroad tracks ahead of an oncoming locomotive as an example to other workers, and was vicious to his legal wife, who unwillingly bore him four children, one of whom was Axel, whom he announced as his heir.

Two other books proved equally disappointing, and the same proved true when Andretta delved into Axel, who owned the house in 1868, the time Derrick Arbiter determined that the bones had been buried in her cellar.

"Next to nothing," Andretta said to Chief Walenski when she and Jamie reported equal disappointment in failing to find any real clue leading to who Minot was. "Both Alquist and his son Axel were perfectly awful people, but that doesn't lead us anywhere except to be shocked by them."

"Perhaps not," the veteran police officer said. Then, he thoughtfully added, "Painting a character picture helps round things out, though. Alquist and Axel are now no longer just names in the fog of history. They have become real people to us. Céline Charlette, for all her glamour, was, in spite of fame and adulation, perhaps a desperate but lonely person, the way many celebrities are. And Alquist's wife was most certainly a helpless woman, powerless and dominated by an abusive husband, with no recourse or hope, as women were at the time. The men? They were both ruthless, viciously cruel, and driven by lust for power and greed. And that leads us to the old standby in every investigation: money."

"Money?" Andretta asked, a little unprepared for the old man's optimism.

"The root of all evil," Walenski said with a laugh. "We know Alquist left his railroad to Axel, along with your house, but what else did he mention in his will? He was very rich. Did Axel get all of it and his half-brother Minot nothing? Maybe, but then maybe not, and if not, who did?

Sometimes even the wording of a will can tell you a host of things. I'll work up a warrant for you to gain access to the probated wills of both Alquist and Axel. Hopefully City Records will still have them in their digital archives or elsewhere. And Jamie will go with you to make the warrant official." He laughed. "Bureaucrats often quail at the sight of a uniform."

And thus Andretta next found herself along with Jamie at an imposing city hall in the heart of Connors Falls, with Jamie in the lead and herself encouraged by Jamie's positive attitude when the young officer laughingly said, "Tracking things down is always good sport, and the way to handle petty officials is to make them feel guilty somehow."

Tracking either Alquist or Axel, however, proved difficult, as well as bending officialdom when faced with a particularly self-righteous official who, in spite of Jamie's convictions, surprisingly felt obliged to make revelation of the wills of both men as difficult as possible, defending his turf with questions as to the exact spelling of names—"How do you spell Mortison?"—and demanding exact dates of death, as well as official residences of both Alquist and Axel, along with their dates of their birth.

It was wearying, and when Andretta and an insistent Jamie were finally given the wills and had the chance to pore over them, they reported back to Chief Walenski, both convinced they had thoroughly wasted their time.

The chief, however, didn't think so, particularly when they reported that Alquist had left every last penny of his wealth to Axel and nothing to Minot or even to Céline Charlette, except a strange bequeathment of an insultingly small one hundred dollars in bonds issued by the Great Lakes and Northern, ten in all and at ten dollars each, which, when cashed, would just enable her to return to France. Axel in turn had willed the whole family fortune to Ezra, who would succeed him as railroad owner, along with the house.

"That's great," Walenski said. "Don't you see what was revealed? He gave nothing to the person we have presumed was his son, and that's Minot. And he insulted his mistress of years with the petty hundred dollars' worth of bonds, a deliberate next-to-nothing compared with all the rest of his fortune.

"In my experience, people getting cut out of wills often harbor deep angry resentments. And more likely than not, Minot did, at the insult to his mother, which I'm sure he saw as equally insulting to himself."

But Jamie, confident in her chief's open trust in her, immediately broke in to say, "You're right, Chief, but if it was enough of an insult to make Minot a killer, it doesn't then make sense to find it's Minot who was buried in Ms. Salinger's cellar. It would have made more sense if the bones belonged to Axel, who inherited everything and was killed by Minot in a rage at being left out of the will, as well as his mother insulted. But that doesn't work because we know Axel remained alive for years after 1868."

"Agreed," said Walenski, reluctantly surrendering. "Which again leaves us where? Who is our murderer?"

Once more, nowhere as usual, Andretta thought, except with both Céline Charlette and Minot storming with rage and resentment at Minot's first being left out of Alquist's will and then almost certain to be disinherited again by Axel.

She stayed a while with the old chief and Jamie, wondering where they'd go next, until Walenski said, "Don't worry. We need time to think. The sole purpose of any homicide investigation is to determine who the killer was, and what was his or her motive. While we're pretty sure of the victim, we're maybe not there yet with his killer, but I'm sure between us we'll come up with something."

Between us? Us? His throwaway words struck Andretta, and brought home how involved she had become with the old man in what seemed almost a partnership, despite her reluctance to be playing detective instead of being an artist and painting. And when she finally left him, it was with a promise to herself that she would come back to him with fresh evidence somehow discovered.

Down in the parking lot, an unpleasant surprise awaited her. Who should she encounter coming to see the police about something or other but Derrick Arbiter, who was all maddeningly put-on cheerful when he said, condescendingly, "Hello, there. Still at it, are you?" his facial expression a virtual sneer.

Andretta fixed on his pretentious bow tie and managed to say, "Yes, thank you," in return.

"I'm sure old Walenski's thinking is 'follow the money,'" Arbiter went on. "It's what in their limited intelligence the cops always do. More likely instead, the old French expression, *Cherchez la femme,* and digging around the railroad baron's scandalous mistress."

With that, and with a supercilious smile of superiority and saying, "I have my findings on a new corpse to discuss," he was gone into the police station, leaving Andretta swept with annoyance and an almost instant depressed feeling that Arbiter in a way represented all the frustrated futility of her failed search for clues that would bring a definite end to the homicide investigation.

The silence of the parking lot as she got out keys for her car was suddenly broken by a voice. "You know something? I think he just might be right."

It was Jamie who had followed her out and, headed for a police car, preparing to go on highway patrol, had been just in time to hear Arbiter. "I know he's impossible," she said. "We have to deal with him all the time. But maybe he's got something there with that *Cherchez la femme* bit. Perhaps we ought to look into it."

Thirteen

And they did. That evening found Jamie joining Andretta in the kitchen of the little stone house, with Andretta, although slightly reluctant to pursue this line of investigation, going along with it. With a mug of coffee pushed to one side, and opening her laptop, Andretta began a search for books or articles about Céline Charlette.

Not really expecting to find any, to her surprise, she did, and in the Harvard library found one in French by someone named Marcel Tavernier, which the computer translated into English for her.

Céline Charlette was born in 1817 in the village of Tourneau sur Marne, east of Paris, near where the Marne River joined the Seine. Skimming, Andretta followed the French girl through early stages of school and village, her singing in regional cabaret stints with her talent and looks leading her to the Moulin Rouge in the Place Pigalle in Paris, and French fame before going to America. There, when performing in the Burlesque, a notorious theater in New York City, she was spotted by Alquist Mortison, and quickly and quite willingly seduced.

"Doesn't get us much, does it," Jamie said, from where she was searching her own laptop on the table next to Andretta, and when told what Andretta had found.

"Just that she was beautiful and one more trophy that Alquist had to have," Andretta said, laughing. It was the end of a day spent searching with their computers, and she was tired but not yet willing to quit. "What have you dredged up?"

"I'm still at the Library of Congress," Jamie said, "and they have quite a pile of stuff. Well, two books, to be exact, both translations from the French. I've just scanned one by her agent and publicity guy, Bernard something, which is just what you would expect. It endlessly extols her professional virtue in one engagement after another from Tourneau sur Marne to New York, with Chicago on the way, and there's another I just started by a someone named Martine Delplice, who apparently was Céline Charlette's dresser for years and her intimate friend. Maybe you'd want to look at that one too."

Andretta pulled up the Library of Congress website, found the book by Martine Delplice, and began reading. The book was badly written, the dresser obviously poorly educated, but it revealed that Céline Charlette had scarce if any use for the then-ailing Alquist, on whom she continued to play her seductive wiles while so furious at his never recognizing his son Minot, whom he held in sneering contempt for being an artist, that she'd secretly cheated on him with his son Axel, even while Alquist was dying.

Both Andretta and Jamie sat back and exchanged looks that neared disbelief: Axel acquiring his father's mistress, who was also the mother of his half-brother Minot? Could such a thing be possible?

Jamie was first to speak. She couldn't help being shocked. "Sick," she said. "Martine Delplice must have it wrong."

"Don't think she does, and it's worse than sick," Andretta argued. "There's no reason to think she's making it up, and it certainly fits somehow. One can hardly think Céline Charlette a nun, and either Axel or his father saints. Read on."

They did, and read that with Alquist unaware of such a disgraceful infidelity, Martine Delplice confirmed that the ageing railroad baron had willed every last penny of his vast fortune to Axel, along with the Great Lakes and Northern railroad.

Andretta, a little behind Jamie, had only just got to that part when she heard a gasp from the young police officer. "What, what?" she demanded, leaving her own laptop to stare at Jamie's.

"Look at this," Jamie said, and Andretta,

crowding close to Jamie, found herself reading Martine Delplice's report of a big fight between Axel and Minot, with Minot threatening to expose a massive fraud by Axel if Axel didn't compensate his mother for the pitiful inheritance Alquist left her. Axel, Delplice wrote, had falsely inflated Great Lakes and Northern's worth to secure huge bank loans to finance a subsequent fraudulent scheme for a highly profitable controlling interest in the Northwestern and Idaho.

"Well, well," Andretta said, leaning back in her chair. "Wouldn't you know it? A big-time crook in the Mortison family."

"Are you surprised?" came from Jamie. "And just as fascinating, an ugly family row over it." She pushed back from the computer in defeat. "But nothing more, so once again, a dead end."

"Maybe not," Andretta said, trying to sound hopeful. "There's an author's footnote in French at the bottom of the page."

Jamie laughed wearily. "I don't read French. What does it say?"

"It says, 'See Professor Auchencloss, *The Freedom Train*, Notes from a Freed Slave, National Archives.'"

"Oh, dear. Paper chase once more," Jamie said. "We all learned about the Freedom Train in school, and the notes are probably just more of the same supporting it." She added sarcastically, "If we're lucky to find it, we probably can read about Axel's big fraud all over again."

Admitting defeat, the two women called it

a day. "Enough for now," Andretta said. They put away their laptops, and had a drink, and said goodnight, and Andretta watched out a window until the blue and red lights on the roof of a police car flashed into the darkness of night, telling her Jamie was on her way home.

Fourteen

Unable to sleep half the night, Andretta caught up by sleeping until mid-morning, when she finally rose, made coffee, unfroze a bagel, and still in her pajamas, sat down at the kitchen table, where she reluctantly opened her laptop and brought up the website of the National Archives and its nonclassified reference section available to the public.

She still had little if any confidence she'd find anything under a Professor Auchencloss, and she acted almost automatically, feeling that just the same, she owed it to both Walenski and Jamie not to leave a job half-finished but to follow any lead, no matter how vague, in the search for the 1868 murderer of the bones unearthed in her cellar.

She finally found Professor Auchencloss and his *Freedom Train* research, a voluminous and endlessly boring work on the flight of slaves northward to freedom before the beginning of the Civil War. None of it told her anything, but eventually she found obscurely buried in it the relatively short section titled "Notes from a Freed Slave."

Why on earth, she wondered, would Martine Delplice have referred to this in her footnote? The notes were virtually illiterate and only a few words each, but all together, as she read, they told of a flight from slavery on a plantation that painted a picture of deprivation, hunger, and terror. One after another, there were brief words like *whipped bad, got free night, men guns chasing, hide long on train, hungry cold* ...

And then, as Andretta was about to give up, something appeared after words indicating the slave's final freedom that sent sudden shivers up her spine. She read, *live rich family.*

Free and living with a rich family? Could that possibly be the Mortisons, and why Martine Delplice footnoted Professor Auchencloss's report, which included the slave's few words? Why else?

Andretta held her beath and then read: *master kill boy, make me bury.*

Fifteen

Arriving at the Connors Falls police station after early road patrol, Jamie was surprised by a call on her cell phone. It was Andretta.

"Guess what, Jamie," she heard Andretta say.

And that was the beginning of euphoria at the police station when Andretta met with the police chief and the young uniformed police officer he'd assigned to help her.

"Wow!" Jamie exclaimed in a sudden burst of excitement when Walenski declared the case closed.

"Wow, indeed, and finally," the police chief said. "It all fits. Arbiter showed us Minot was murdered, Delplice wrote about Minot's threat to reveal Axel's giant fraud, and now, finally, that poor slave saying it was Axel who killed Minot. Quite obviously, we know, to keep him quiet about his fraud."

"And that's all of it," Walenski added "Yes, the why, the how, and who was responsible."

But Andretta was speechless. It was all so sudden, the end of weeks of nagging curiosity and discomfort. Yes, the how, the why and finally the who of the bones in her cellar had finally been discovered, but instead of the elation and relief she was supposed to feel, she instead experienced an unexpected kind of emptiness, a feeling that she was in a no-man's-land, one in which she no longer pursued a murder nor peacefully enjoyed living in her little stone house and painting in the barn.

She found it hard to join in the elation the police chief also felt. "Axel Mortison's guilt," Walenski said, "proves what I thought, that it would come down to money, one way or another. It always does in nearly every case of homicide, and this one proved no exception."

But did it? Andretta tried to keep up a pretense of delight within herself as well as with others. Was chasing down the murderer of bones buried in her cellar finally over? Really? Reluctantly, she forced herself to quell her vague misgivings as being without reason.

Walenski's conviction helped her to do so. After all, she brought herself to think, Walenski was a police officer, and the police chief at that. He had to be right. Asserting a kind of unwilling self-discipline, she surrendered herself to settling down and resuming a normal routine with the Marker brothers returning to redo her cellar and herself getting back to work on the big abstract in her barn.

Often, however, and in spite of her determination, she'd feel a nagging return of uneasiness, of the feeling that something was missing, something to perhaps put an emphatic closure to what her life had become in the past several months.

Her unsettled feeling continued until one rather chilly early autumn day when she was in her barn finishing up the last work on her big abstract, and she became aware of a police car as it came to a stop on Holway Road by her mail box. And the next thing she knew, she had welcome company.

"Hi, Andretta. Sneaking a break."

It wasn't the first time Jamie had appeared so abruptly on the lonely Holway Road. A bond of friendship had formed between Andretta and the young uniformed police officer during the homicide investigation, and Jamie, who loved art and was fascinated by its creation, often stopped by. She was the only person Andretta would tolerate in her barn while she worked.

"Hey," Jamie said. "How can you paint? Aren't you freezing?"

Andretta laughed, and stepped back to eye the abstract critically before putting down brush and palette. She was indeed beginning to get cold. Summer was over and the air had a sense of oncoming frost.

"Yes," she said. "And it's late coffee hour, and

I've been waiting to be rescued."

"Sure you have time?" Andretta asked, after they had reached the kitchen of the house and, coffee ready, was getting down mugs.

"My time's my own on back-country patrol," Jamie said. She grinned conspiratorially. "Who's to know where I am?"

Andretta led the way to the small living room she'd furnished with a new sofa and a low coffee table before a fireplace. She lit a fire she'd laid earlier, and she and Jamie settled on the couch with coffee and talked, each bringing the other up to date on their respective daily lives.

"And the chief?" Andretta asked.

"Thinking of retirement."

Andretta mentally pictured the aging police chief, and how worn out he'd looked when she'd last seen him, and said, "He should, the poor old guy. Had enough, I guess."

Jamie suddenly became oddly silent, and Andretta noticed she was almost absently staring at the wall above the mantlepiece of the fireplace.

"What?" she asked.

"The blank space above the mantlepiece," Jamie said. "Isn't that space in most houses usually filled with art of some sort, like a favorite painting?"

"I don't have anything small enough to do the trick," Andretta said.

"Yes, you do. What about your little railroad Collage? All those trains and news headlines and people and that huge wonderful locomotive coming right out at you, cowcatcher and all. Why is it still hanging in the kitchen?"

The question took Andretta completely by surprise, and she realized that all through the homicide investigation, in which the collage had played such a major part, she'd become so used to it hanging in the kitchen that she'd never thought of hanging it any place else, especially above the fireplace in the living room, a room so rarely used in the summer months.

"I'll go get it," Jamie said, and before Andretta could think twice, she did just that, abruptly leaving the comfort of sitting before the fire and reappearing moments later with the collage.

"Want to give it a try?" she demanded, laughing, and without waiting for Andretta to reply, she held the collage against the bare wall over the mantle. "How does it look?"

Andretta stared. It was perfect. Why hadn't she ever thought of it? She said so, and Jamie said, "Good—I'll do it for you, but I'll need a hammer and a nail to hang it from."

"Careful," Andretta said, "the frame's pretty old and shaky."

"Right," Jamie said, but even as she turned from the mantle with the collage, she exclaimed, "Oops! Think something broke off."

She gently laid the collage face down on the coffee table and said, "I felt one of the rusty little clips holding on the back come loose."

"Here it is, on the floor," Andretta said, bending to retrieve the metal clip. Half rusted away, it was one of two used to hold backing onto the collage.

"Gosh, I'm sorry," Jamie said. "Must have snagged it with a finger, and look, it nearly took off the backing with it too."

Then both women went silent a moment as they stared at a sheet of ancient thin cardboard used to secure the collage itself in the frame and which had slipped halfway out.

Andretta was first to speak. "What the hell?" She pulled the cardboard sheet free, exposing not the backs of coal-burning locomotives with their huge cowcatchers and smoke pouring from their high funnels, with one giant locomotive dominating all, but something so different that for a moment it silenced both her and Jamie. Covering the collage was a sheet of ten very faded certificates of bonds issued by the Great Lakes and Northern Railroad.

"What on earth is all that?" Jamie finally asked.

"Bonds," Andretta said, looking closely. "Ten of them at ten bucks each. And issued in 1860."

"What are bonds?"

"They're loans issued by companies to borrow money from investors. These are their printed certificates."

"Are they worth anything?"

Andretta laughed. "Unfortunately not even five cents today, except maybe a few bucks to an antique dealer. They were even made worthless by 1870 when Great Lakes and Northern was sold."

"But what on earth are they doing there?" Jamie said.

Andretta tried to think. They had to have been placed there by Minot. Who else? And Andretta found herself imagining the young artist doing so, herself there with him and watching along with his mother Céline Charlette. But why, why?

And suddenly she knew and could feel why. As a fellow artist, she could feel and know exactly how she was certain Minot had felt. She found herself with him and the collage as he fixed the bonds to its back, could feel and see his utter disdain for his paltry inheritance. She could feel that amidst all his anger at the insult to himself and his mother that the bonds represented, the young artist chose to reject their money value by not cashing them but instead was thumbing his nose at Alquist by defiantly making them part of his art that both Alquist and his son, Axel, were so contemptuous of.

"They'll stay right where they are," Andretta said.

While she fetched a hammer and a nail, Jamie took a photo of the bonds with her phone to give to Police Chief Walenski. "Aside from his being a cop," she said, "the old boy will appreciate seeing them. This case meant so much to him."

Andretta agreed, and after applying duct tape—"until I can get the whole collage more safely framed"—to refix the thin cardboard that had come away from its back, she and Jamie hung the work again over the mantlepiece and then sat down on the couch to admire it.

"I could look at that great locomotive charging at me all day," Jamie said, and even as Jamie spoke, Andretta finally felt the elusive closure to the discovery of the bones in her cellar, which for so long had evaded her. Minot's defiance had done that, and she at once decided she would see the bones given a funeral and properly buried when police officialdom was fully done with its investigation.

"End of story," she said to Jamie, with a deep feeling of relief and content, and fixed them both a drink while Jamie put in a routine call to the police station to say she'd ended patrol and had nothing to report.

Except the story wasn't ended. Not quite.

On a cold late autumn day several weeks later, when Andretta had put finishing touches to the big abstract she'd worked on for so long, and had brought all her art material to the house, and had shut the barn for the winter, she was taking a break in her kitchen when her cell phone rang. Vaguely annoyed at any interruption to setting up for work in her living room, and wondering who it was, she answered.

"Hello? Who's this?"

"Who" was Police Chief Walenski. He was brief. "Ms. Salinger, sorry, but it's about bones again. There's been an unexpected turn in the investigation, and if possible, I'd appreciate your coming to my office."

Sixteen

"You'll forgive me," the old police chief said, after Andretta had been shown into his office by an oddly excited Jamie, who was obviously holding back something so her chief could speak first.

"I took the liberty to act on your behalf when Jamie here sent me a photograph she took of the 1860 bond issue you discovered on the back of the collage you have hanging in your house." He paused for a moment and broke into an unexpected smile. "I have a surprise for you, Ms. Salinger."

Jamie burst out laughing and Walenski, his own smile broadening, said, "On a vague hunch, I took the photo to Terrance, Reilly and Lee, and after a while they came up with the bonds still being negotiable today, with the Union Pacific being liable, having bought them along with Northwestern and Idaho, who'd acquired them from Great Lakes and Northern. They also acknowledged that your possible suit for the bonds' value would not be worth the cost of their defending. On today's market, that value is a little more than a million and a half dollars."

In the following days, when the outburst of euphoria finally died down and Andretta overcame her astonishment, she would hear nothing but to divide the million and a half dollars between herself and the three others who had so earnestly sought, along with her, to find the identity of the bones discovered buried in her cellar, as well as who had buried them and when and why. So, equal shares of wealth went, besides to herself, to Police Chief Tom Walenski, to police officer Jamie Smith, and not without considerable reluctance, to the anthropology pathologist Derrick Arbiter.

Where are they all now?

Chief Walenski retired and used his share to build and promote a small police history wing at the Conrors Falls museum. Jamie, while remaining a close friend of Andretta, stayed a cop, a job she loved, with her share as a nest egg and with part of it used to buy Andretta's painting *Blue,* which she so loved and insisted on paying for. And Derrick Arbiter used his share to support himself while authoring a lengthy scientific work on the continued influence of adverse genetics on irregular monocular structure after death.

Andretta? As a proud citizen of the town of Connors Falls, and while becoming more and more widely known as an artist, she used nearly all of her share to buy hundreds of acres of fields and woodland around her little stone house for a wildlife refuge, the love of which she shared in a few years' time in marriage with an author of historical fiction.

The tourist pamphlet on a haunted house is no longer in the Connors Falls fast-food diner's "Things to See" rack. However, a carefully photographed copy of the reframed collage that now hangs over the mantlepiece in the living room of 24 Holway Road is displayed prominently in the Connors Falls public library, along with a complete history of its creation and the role it played in revealing the town's most notorious homicide, which occurred in 1868.

End

About the Author

 David Osborn, for over sixty years a writer, lives in Connecticut with his wife, a once American and European ballerina, then renowned in international health policy. Their daughter, a PhD psychologist, practices in Sydney, Australia. Their lawyer son is an advocate for the welfare of animals worldwide.

Also by David Osborn

Novels and Screenwriting

Novels

The Glass Tower – Hodder & Stoughton
Open Season – The Dial Press
The French Decision – Doubleday
Love and Treason – New American Library
Heads – Bantam
Murder on Martha's Vineyard – Lynx
Murder on the Chesapeake – Simon & Schuster
Murder in the Napa Valley – Simon & Schuster
The Last Pope – Source Books
The Cape Cod Blue – Dagmar Miura
Alicia's Secret (young adult) – Dagmar Miura
A Cold Wind from the Andes – Dagmar Miura
The Head Hunters – Dagmar Miura
Looking Back: The Long Life of a Writer (a memoir)
Delta Red – Dagmar Miura
Eventide – Dagmar Miura
The Somersville Bodies – Dagmar Miura
Cold Case 369 – Dagmar Miura
The Lighthouse (a novella)– Dagmar Miura
The Saugatuck Conspiracy – Dagmar Miura
Bones – Dagmar Miura

For Children

Jessica and the Crocodile Knight (a novel) – HarperCollins

Jessica and Her Adventures in Fairyland (collection of five novellas) – Dagmar Miura

Ophelia and Her Forest Friends (series of ten stories) – Dagmar Miura

Jessica and the Witch's Broom – Dagmar Miura

Jessica and the Flying Unicorns – Dagmar Miura

Jessica and the Golden Swan Feather – Dagmar Miura

Feature Films

The Trap (original story and screenplay; Academy Award nominee for Best Foreign Film) – Columbia

Open Season (screenplay, adapted from Osborn's own best-selling novel *Open Season*) – Columbia

Chase a Crooked Shadow (original story and screenplay co-written with Charles Sinclair; listed by the British Academy of Motion Picture Science as "One of the ten best suspense scripts ever written") – Warner Bros.

Moment of Danger, a.k.a. *Malaga* (screenplay adapted from the novel) – Warner Bros.

Malaga (screenplay) – Warner Bros.

Maroc 7 (original story and screenplay) – J. Arthur Rank

Deadlier Than the Male (original story and screenplay) – J. Arthur Rank

Some Girls Do (original story and screenplay) – J. Arthur Rank

The Road to Dusty Death (screenplay) – J. Arthur Rank

The Games (screenplay) – Associated British

Follow the Boys (original story and screenplay) – MGM

Beat Girl (original story and screenplay) – Renown Films/British Lion

Stop-over Forever (original story and screenplay) – British Lion

Winter Holiday (original story and screenplay) – MGM

Penny Gold (original story and screenplay) – J. Arthur Rank/Columbia

Whoever Slew Auntie Roo? (original story and screenplay) – Paramount & American International

Murder, She Said (screenplay, Agatha Christie adaptation) – MGM

Murder at the Gallop (screenplay, Agatha Christie adaptation) – MGM

Feature-Length Documentaries

Fangio, The History of Formula One Racing (original screenplay; executive producer) – Volpi Productions

Why Ireland – Irish Tourist Bureau

Films Canceled While in Production

HMS Ulysses – Volpi Productions (screenplay adaptation of the Alistair MacLean novel about protecting North Sea convoys to Russia during World War II; production halted when a key warship was unavailable)

The Mad Motorists – Volpi Productions (screenplay adaptation from the Allen Andrews novel about the 1907 Peking to Paris race)

Eagle at Sundown – Dragon Films (original screen story about Napoleon's escape from Elba; starring Douglas Fairbanks; in production when canceled)

Les Petits Rats – Disney (original story and screenplay about the Paris Ballet school; production begun, then canceled)

Hunters' Horn – McCahon Productions (screenplay adaptation from the Harriette Simpson Arnow novel; production canceled; financing failure)

Blood on the Rose – British Lion (screenplay adaptation from the Phyllis Hastings novel)

Television

Bouquet for Miss Olive (three-act play; British Television Producers Association nominee for Best Play of the Year) – Granada/ITV

Three on a Gas Ring (three-act play; British Television Producers Association nominee for Best Play of the Year) – Granada/ITV

Why George Brown Hanged (three-act play) –
    Granada/ITV

Arthur of the Britons (pilot and three scripts on
    the life of King Arthur; Writers Guild of
    Great Britain award winner for Best British
    Children's Series)

The Antiquers (original story, pilot, and six
    episodes in the sitcom series) – Irish National
    Television